MindGap

The following is an exclusive imprint of Summer House Publishing

and Summer House Media LLC

www.summerhousepublishing.co

For rights, literary requests or other inquiries, please contact Chris Varonos at:

chris@summerhousemedia.co

Cover and interior design by Nuno Moreira, NM DESIGN

ISBN: 978-1-7372920-1-2

MindGap

a story by

BEN MANHAN

"Life would be tragic if it weren't funny."

— Stephen Hawking

My stomach turns and pushes acid into my throat. I'm not sure if it's from the whiskey I've been guzzling or this guy's driving. I'm pretty sure he's been asking me questions the whole ride, but thankfully it's impossible to hear through the machine-gun patter of rain outside and the static-ridden radio he has turned up way too loud. The cab peels right around a corner and I must press my hand down to avoid sliding across the seat. My knees clench the precious brown bag between them. His brakes must be in mint condition, but the interior is far from it. The worn-down faux leather has so many stains it almost looks like a pattern print. The heater is blasting so much that the air has become thick and humid. I'm being driven around in a sweaty boot. It smells like it too. It's times like these I wish I could afford a limo. I try to roll down my window, but it doesn't budge. Damn it.

"Can I roll down the window?" I ask.

"What's that, Pete?" he says.

I've spent my entire life telling people there's an "r" at the end of my name.

"It's Peter."

"Turn up the heater?"

"No! The fucking window!"

"I can't hear you."

He turns down the radio.

"Can you unlock my window?"

"So we drown? No thanks. Not sure where you're from, but we don't have the luxury of driving with the windows down. Sorry, Pete."

He cranks up the radio.

"I don't have the luxury to breathe!"

"Did ya say something?" he yells.

I can't take this anymore. The cork lid comes off my whiskey bottle with a pop, and I put the brown bag to my lips. Like getting punched in the stomach, it doesn't hurt until you breathe. I blow the fire out of my throat, and the caterpillars in the mirror jump. The radio goes down again.

"Whoa, whoa, you can't drink in here, my friend. I can lose my license."

I wipe my mouth with the back of my hand and push the cork back in.

"I was thirsty."

"I've heard that before. You gotta be careful with that stuff, my friend. I lost my cousin to the bottle. Young guy too . . . lots of potential, but that stuff will get ya. He came to Seattle for school, to become a doctor. Smart kid. It's a real shame, my aunt was so torn up. Breaks my heart to think about. Funeral was sad."

"Aren't all funerals sad?" I ask.

He shrugs off the question and rifles through his pockets. It smells like something's burning. Jesus, he lit a fucking cigarette. I try the window again. Still locked. Holding my breath, I look out through the windshield and see the faint tungsten glow of the streetlamps I know all too well. We've arrived.

"Tell me where's good." He puffs.

"Just pull over here."

"Where?"

"Here!"

He slams on the brakes with a fifty-pound foot and I catch myself on his seat. I pay him, grab my bottle, and kick the door open. The rain is roaring. I step onto the concrete and stare at my feet, a minor obstacle to the water that is racing off the sides, just as the architect had designed it.

"Hey, you're not gonna jump, are ya, Pete?"

The driver has his window rolled down with his cigarette hanging out of his mouth.

"Excuse me?" I ask.

"Look, buddy, I don't know you and I don't want to judge. But you got the bottle there and this bridge has a history of sorts, ya know? You just got all the makings and, I don't know. I don't wanna read in the paper tomorrow that somethin' happened and I coulda stopped it, ya know? I can't be all feeling like it was my responsibility. Couldn't live with it. Don't do that to me, man."

My fist clenches. I press the bottle to my lips and take a gulp of fire. I lean down so I can look him in the eye.

"Listen, you stinky prick. You don't know a goddamn thing about this bridge. All that shit you read in the papers, that isn't reality. It's a heartless, parasitic form of storytelling with no regard for what life truly feels like at times. It may be what helps you pass the time when you're not sucking on that cancer stick driving a sweaty boot around, but trust me, pal, you couldn't fucking stop me even if you tried."

I quickly reach for the cigarette, but he leans back, throws the car into drive, and blows smoke into my face. The tires spin in place before they catch, and he peels out.

"Yeah, smell you later!" I shout.

What starts as small polka dots on my sweatpants quickly becomes a dark gray dampness. The rain clinks against the neck of the bottle as I take a swig from the bag, breathe fire, and wipe my mouth with my wrist. Unlike your typical suspension bridge, the Aurora is just a flat cantilever and truss running from Queen Anne to Fremont. I lean over the railing and watch the pouring rain fall past me, down into the darkness below. A true black hole. A way out. I think about it every time I'm here. Everyone does. Whether they're on a rooftop, a bridge, a cliff. It has nothing to do with being suicidal. I think it's more of human nature trying to comprehend how vulnerable we really are. Curiosity is the word. Those thoughts scare most people, but to me they're soothing. It's like a fucked-up form of meditation. I find some peace in knowing there's always an escape.

My eyes dart to the rattling suicide-prevention sign hanging in the wind. Every time I come here, I think of my brother. I was standing right here. I can still picture him in his beige raincoat that hung below his knees. His glasses kept fogging up, so he would wipe them on his shirt. And his clean-cut hair just laid flat. He was calm as always, like everything had already been calculated. Nothing seemed to be bothering him. We talked for a while, and I just listened. I never moved. Not even when the conversation ended. I spent three years trying to understand how he made it look so easy, like stepping off a curb. The little green man gave him the "okay" and he just walked off. I don't have the courage Kevin did. But pretending I do is what clears my head. It helped me write the only project I've ever actually finished, my novel about him, *Invisible Pain*. The book's existence still brings inner conflict: the mild commercial success I received came with a forever pit of guilt in my stomach of knowing I'm a talentless hack that could only eclipse mediocrity on the back of my dead brother. Can I even claim to have writer's block if I was never really a writer in the first place?

I bring the bottle back to my lips and breathe fire. This is the closest I can get to Kevin nowadays, so I come here when I'm stuck. I try to put myself in his shoes in that moment, but I never quite get there. I feel the ground of the last place he existed in the world. In my world. He was by far my biggest fan, and, considering our parents' rejection of writing as a viable career path, probably my only familial fan. Whenever I got stuck, he was always the one to help me by asking intelligent questions, poking holes in plots, throwing random thoughts at me until something clicked in my head. Kevin the golden child could do no wrong. My parents will tell you. They always compared me to him. He was the son they dreamed of: Kevin the doctor. Genius at birth. Even he noticed our parents' unequal love bias and always tried to be on my side, even in his final moments.

You used to be able to stick your head out and see the water below, but now the chain-link fence is in the way. It's been despicably nicknamed the "Weak Link Fence," rubbing pounds of salt in my guilt-filled wounds. He wasn't weak, he was exactly the opposite. Fucking morons. No wonder it's covered in graffiti and hateful slurs.

I look up to the top, knowing someone with one atom of athletic ability could just climb over it anyway. Harder than stepping off a curb, sure, but no match for human determination. I bring the fire back to my lips. It burns. This time I don't even bother wiping, since the rain is doing it for me. Then the roar of an engine, and a wave of oily water crashes on top of me.

"What the fuck!" I spit out a mouthful. "Fuckin' asshole!"

I chuck my bottle at the car but the glass crunches against the road. The taillights are gone. Fuck. I'm so thirsty.

I cross the bridge and head down the avenue. This used to be a nice area, but over the years it slowly became a war zone. The fight for turf between the transients and the hookers. I can't imagine being in either position. One trades their dignity for money, the other their body. Both selling their souls. In the end, no one wins. Welcome to the American Dream.

Dim lights, hazy air, and a crowd of regulars pack a dive bar. I sit on an empty stool at the far end and wait to be noticed. The bartender is a young guy chatting it up with some middle-aged woman that looks like an ad to quit smoking. My eyes grab his and won't let go. He tells her, "One sec," then walks over.

"What can I get you?"

"Whiskey. Neat."

"Sounds good. You wanna open a tab?"

I hand him my credit card. He looks it over, then taps it on the wood counter.

"One whiskey, comin' right up, Pete." He winks.

A couple sorority-looking girls come in and take his attention. Girls like that never liked me. I was a ghost to them. They think their looks will last forever, but in ten years they'll wish they picked me over some jock whose belly is so big he needs to stand on a mirror to see his own dick. The bartender grabs a glass, flips it in the palm of his hand, tosses it behind his back, and catches it on the other side. He places it on the bar while it spins like a top and he pours a stream of whiskey, slowly lifting the bottle higher until he drops it down for the finale. The bottle is holstered into the bar, and the glass stops with a gentle karate chop. I hope he doesn't do this circus act every damn pour or I'll never finish the bottle before close.

"Enjoy. Let me know if you need anything else." He shoots

a finger at me and turns toward the girls.

"Wait."

In one motion, the glass locks onto my lips and the brown water is shot into the back of my throat.

"Another," I croak.

He smiles and nods. "No prob." He pours, looking back at the girls, smiling.

The second he lifts the bottle my hand is already on the glass. My throat burns before he can set it down.

"Another," I demand. He cocks an eyebrow.

"How about I just leave the bottle?" He holds it out.

My determination to finish this bottle has made my aim worse. What went from a few dribbles down my chin has become a soaking-wet cologne on my shirt. That's if it even gets close to my mouth. Some of these shots have gone right over my shoulder and onto the floor. It must've been more than I realized because the bartender put up a WET FLOOR sign behind me. That's the only recognition I've gotten from him since he gave me the bottle. That jerk has been flirting with those college girls the whole time. He's just doing it because it's his job to, not because he wants to. He's just leading them on like a coward. I'll show them what a real man is. Like a Newton's cradle, my feet take turns getting me across the bar until I make it to the girls.

"Hey, ladies."

They turn.

"Ew. Go away, creep."

"C'mon, I'm sure you're sick of this juggling act bothering

you." I take a swig, making eye contact with the bartender.

"He's my boyfriend, asshole," one says.

"This asshole?" I point at him with the butt of the bottle.

"Okay, I think you've had enough," the bartender says, and reaches for my medicine.

"No! I'm almost done."

I take another big swig and lose my balance. I fall onto the bartender's girlfriend and we both topple to the floor. She's screaming in my ear.

"Hey, Ronny, get this clown out of here!" the bartender yells.

Some big guy helps me to my feet. What a gentleman.

"It's time to go, pal."

"Let me finish my drink . . ."

I go to take another sip, but he grabs the bottle from me.

"You've had enough."

"Hey! That's mine!"

He grabs my collar and drags me toward the door.

"Let me go!" I fight for the bottle.

He throws me outside and I stumble onto my ass.

"Piss off," he spits.

As he turns around, I leap for the bottle but miss and land on his feet. I reach up for it; it's just within reach. My fingers can almost touch it. He picks me up by my shirt. I'm still reaching, so close.

"Let me finish it. I can finish it, I swear."

In slow motion, I see his massive fist coming straight for my face.

•

The rain has washed away most of the whiskey on my shirt. My eye is throbbing, and I can feel my brain pulsating against my temples. I stumble to my feet and briefly succeed in one of the greatest balancing acts in history, glancing into a shop window that reflects the puffy darkness forming around my eye. I look pathetic. This is the image my parents had of me. A drunk who couldn't even finish anything, better yet a bottle of whiskey. I'm a fucking loser. My dad was right. He can't be right. He's an asshole. My eyes feel so hot. It's impossible to tell what's rain and what's tears. I can't remember the last time I cried. My knees buckle and I collapse on the cold, wet concrete.

"I . . . I need help, Kev! Kev . . . please! You know I don't beg. I've never begged. I've never even prayed! There's nothing for me to pray to! If you want me to get on my knees and pray to a creator like he's some real thing then I'll do it, but just know I'm doing it for you. God might not be real, but you are. That's why I need you, Kevin. I need something, anything to show me there's a reason for all this. I'm struggling and I just want to let go. Help me let go! If there is a God out there, give me what I want! Just fucking help me!"

A blinding light shines down from above, forcing me to shield my eyes.

"*Hello, Peter,*" a deep voice calls.

"Kev? Kev, is that you?" I scream.

Under my forearm I peek through to see the light emanating

from a massive hologram billboard.

"*Feeling overwhelmed?*"

"Yes," I whimper.

"*Finding it hard to enjoy life?*"

"Yes!"

"*Let us help you, Peter.*"

"How do you know my name?"

The white light shifts to a deep neon blue. White pixels begin swirling in the center and connecting to each other with electronic impulses. I stare at the glowing particles as they form what looks like a microchip. I reach out, but my hand goes right through the hologram.

"What . . . what is it?"

"*This is MindGap. The answer to all your problems.*"

A holographic image of myself appears and I stumble back on my ass into a pile of trash bags. The projection of myself has a disturbing smile across its face. I grab a beer bottle from the trash and hurl it at my uncanny reflection. The bottle flies right through my holographic skull and shatters on the billboard, intertwining with the rain and falling back down on me. For a split second I'm pulled from reality, all my issues torn away by the remnants of the beer bottle. I watch the jubilant Peter fade away, throwing a wink just before he disappears as I shield myself from the debris. Something sharp catches my neck and I find blood on my palm as I feel for it. All that's left of the sign is the smoky mist and, behind it, red and blue flashing lights. An officer approaches me, talking into his shoulder.

"We got a bum vandalizing private property."

"I'm not a bum, I'm a writer."

"What's the difference?" He clicks the handcuffs on.

This cruiser makes me miss the cab. That stink-mobile was much better than these plastic seats. The handcuffs are digging into my wrists and my bony ass on top isn't helping.

"Can you just take me home? We're not too far from my apartment."

"Quiet," he snaps.

"Dick."

He slams on the brakes and my nose cracks against the plexiglass divider. Blood warms my lip.

This cell smells worse than the taxi. It's cold yet somehow humid. Like that one time I left my sock in the fridge. There's another guy here that looks too comfortable for it to be his first time. He flashes a nefarious smile at me, which even if I wanted to reciprocate I couldn't because my face is numb and swollen.

An officer approaches the door.

"Peter Mitchell."

"That's me." I stand up.

"Your bail has been posted."

"Already? By whom?"

The moment I step outside, a black SUV rolls up.

"Peter Mitchell?" says a soothing female voice from inside the car.

"Yeah?"

The back door opens. I cautiously approach and trip off the

curb. No one is inside. Not even a driver.

"Please come with me."

"Uh, who said that?"

"I did," the car says.

That checks out. I lean inside and see a blue under-glow around a mini bar with decanters of all colors. Bingo. Brown liquor in a glass decanter is enough for me to overlook the mysterious autonomous vehicle that may or may not have posted my bail. Sure, decision making isn't my finest trait, but what more do I have to lose?

We've been driving for at least an hour now, far from the Space Needle and deep into the dense Washington forest. The towering western hemlocks stare down at us disapprovingly as trespassers to their world. I understand their anger, but they need to learn not to judge so harshly. My book barely sold any physical copies so they're lucky to be alive. We finally pull off the highway and down a narrow dirt road. I should be more concerned than I am, but perhaps the re-up of brown medicine from this crystal glass has silenced any worry. We arrive at a large, army-green gate. A beam of light scans the entire car before the gate slowly opens. The path continues through a landscape of perfectly placed boulders and junglelike foliage. It stops at a flight of concrete steps leading up to the most unique architecture I've ever seen. If a Bond villain had a villain, then this is where they'd live. Tucked between the large trees sits a building composed of three concrete cubes—the smallest being the entrance, sitting in front of the medium-size cube.

The third is larger than both of them combined and stands adjacent to the first two. The foundation, also concrete, plays as a podium displaying this magnificent structure. Large slats of stained wood surround windows, corners, and, from what I can see, the entire top. The roof hangs out about two feet, providing a nice cover while adding complementary shadows to the building's lines.

The car door opens, so I get out, drink in hand, and climb the steps. It's even bigger up close. I get to the front door, which looks like steel. Let's see if it feels like steel too.

"Stop," a voice booms.

I freeze like a statue. As if a banged-up mop-headed statue would exist here. Another red light scans my body head to toe.

"Welcome, Peter."

The door slowly peels open. The entrance is huge, like something out of a sci-fi movie where everything in the future is pearl white. Without windows or any visible light source, every surface in this room emits some sort of glow.

"Right this way," says a woman who comes out of nowhere. Or the door behind her.

"Oh, thank God. A human. Where am I?" I ask.

She doesn't respond, continuing toward a door in the distance. I follow her through it into an elevator, spotless and whiter than my teeth. I can't tell if we're going up or down but we're definitely moving. We stop. The door splits open into what looks like a therapist's office made of porcelain. All the furniture—except the desk that might be glass or lavish plastic—is white. I step out and the woman stays in the elevator as the doors close behind me. There's an older woman sitting in a chair. She's thin like me, but it looks good on her. Her dark black hair complements her fair skin and space black pantsuit. I feel like a slob.

"Hello, Peter. Please have a seat wherever you feel comfortable."

I'm wet, bleeding, and dirty, so I try to find a piece of furniture that I can't ruin too much. No luck, so I just sit on the shiny couch.

"Who are you? And what is this place?" I ask.

She stands up and begins pacing around the room. Mostly around me. I'm trying to follow her but she keeps going behind me and I have to jerk my head from side to side. On her last go-around she grabs my drink and stops where I can't see her. Before I can retort she speaks.

"Why are you here?"

I try to turn but can't get my head around.

"Um, you tell me. You bailed me out of jail?"

"So why are you here?"

"Why did you bring me here?"

"Why did you destroy my billboard?"

"Oh . . . that was yours. Now I get it. I'm sorry; it was just an accident."

"You accidentally threw a glass bottle at my billboard?"

She comes around, back in front of me. Then faces away.

"Look, I can pay you for it. I have some money."

I reach for my wallet but don't feel it in any of my pockets. I start to panic.

"One point two million dollars," she says as she flashes my wallet. "I already checked. Two hundred is close but not enough."

"I'll have to sell way more books. My first one barely broke a fraction of that."

She heads for her desk and sits down. She pulls out a glass tablet and stylus, then swivels her chair around, facing away from me again.

"Why don't you tell me about that?" She grips her stylus. "What was it about? Your first book."

"My brother."

"Kevin, correct?"

"Yeah . . ."

"Do you still think about your brother a lot?"

"Well, yeah. Yes, I do."

"Why he killed himself?"

"More like how."

"It takes a lot to get to that point."

"And yet he made it look so easy."

"And you wish you could do it too, don't you? But you can't muster the courage like he did."

I stand up in a rage.

"Who the fuck are you? Asking me all these questions like you know my life. You're not my fucking therapist. I don't need this shit!"

"Have you ever been to therapy, Peter?"

"Fuck no! Nobody understands me besides me. I'm an enigma. That's why I write!"

"How's your second book coming along?"

I open my mouth, but nothing comes out.

"Therapy isn't only for people with depression, Peter. You're telling me there's nothing bothering you? Not a single thing about yourself you wish you could fix?" She glares at me.

"I don't know."

"Do you remember the last thing you finished? Could be as simple as a chore like laundry, or a puzzle. Anything you can think of?"

"I . . . I don't remember."

"Your parents. Are they still alive?"

"I think so."

"You don't speak to them?"

"No. They sued me."

She writes something down. I continue.

"They didn't like my book about Kevin. Thought I used his death to turn a profit."

"What is your new book about?"

"I hate that question."

"Is it a comedy? A tragedy?"

"My life or the book?"

She circles something with her stylus, not even a slight smile at my joke. I thought that was pretty funny. My self-amusement is all that matters.

"What's your apartment like? Is it clean, messy, somewhere

in between?" she asks.

"Uh, I'd say it's pretty clean. It's how I like it."

"You like having dirty laundry on your couch?"

"What?"

"Your coffee table is covered in books you told yourself you'd read but only got halfway through. It's clear from the bookmarks."

"Did you—"

"Your refrigerator has a shopping list that's been there for months, but nothing is checked off. Your dining table is full of pieces from puzzles you aren't even sure which belong to what anymore. Your TV stand is moving boxes you've been meaning to unpack for a year now. Do I need to continue?"

"No. I get it."

"Peter, you're stuck. Stuck in a place in your life that you feel you can't get out of. You've bombarded yourself with tasks and desires you want to achieve, but have extended your reach far too wide to put the time it takes into accomplishing any of them. This is not uncommon these days. Every day our brains are becoming more overwhelmed by the amount of information we're being exposed to. Technology is evolving so quickly that we can barely keep up with it. Technology can be a fantastic tool, but now our tools have tools. We can only handle so much of this, and you've seemed to arrive at a place where grief hangs like a raincloud over your day-to-day life. To cope, you overwhelm your brain to the point of inoperability. It's overstimulated on purpose, albeit unconsciously. Your actions are self-destructive, but not entirely intentional. It's a sickness.

It's like a mold that grows only in the shadows. The shadow of your lost brother, a man who externally exuded excellence and contentment, but internally battled the deadliest of demons. Invisible pain. We all have some. You need your brain to learn how to keep up with the pace of the current world."

I begin crying uncontrollably. My emotions flood out of me like a dam has broken inside.

"What do I do?"

"Do you trust me?"

She stands up and motions me toward the door. I definitely don't trust her, but what choice do I have? I follow her blindly.

We get in the same elevator. She waves a fob across a plate on the wall, and we start moving. The elevator stops and opens directly into another room. "Room" is actually an understatement. This looks like an entire building of its own. We're inside a tall, glossy white cylinder, I'd guess at least three stories high. A spiral staircase coils the walls of the narrow room all the way to the top. Like looking down the barrel of a gun. Windows are tiled here and there in the same configuration. The floor is one solid piece that's so shiny it looks wet. I can only imagine how slippery this thing can get. Or how squeaky new shoes would be against it. I follow her toward the back wall where the stairs begin. As we get closer, I realize these aren't normal stairs. There's just a single step, or platform. She steps on it.

"What are you waiting for?" she asks.

I stand next to her. The platform starts ascending the spiral track. I'm convinced that the elevator is a time machine. As we pass the tiled windows, I notice each are individual rooms. Surgery rooms, they look like. Almost all of them are occupied by a doctor and a seated patient. We keep moving up the spiral until we reach the top. The top section is an entire floor to itself. All I can think about is how shitty my apartment is compared to this place.

She gets off first, swipes her fob, and the door opens with a hiss. The ceiling is low, like we're in a bunker, though to be honest I still have no clue whether we're above or below ground. Unlike the doctors' offices leading up here, this room is empty save for a single, tilted-back chair in the center.

"Please have a seat. This will answer any questions you have."

I sit down and lie back against the chair. This reminds me of a planetarium I went to once. You recline in a chair like this, angled toward the ceiling, while stars and planets are projected above you.

Suddenly, the room drops into pitch black. I turn around but not even a sliver of light leaks in. I've never experienced something this dark. It's almost like my eyes have been removed from my head. If it wasn't for this chair, I would have completely lost my sense of direction. A small green light appears in front of me. It slowly grows and expands into thousands of little particles. Like a school of fish, the particles move together, taking the shape of a ribbon. They change from green to red, then to blue then purple. They slowly fade back to complete darkness. In an instant, the entire room lights up, but it looks nothing like it did before. The ceiling is no longer low. It looks like I'm staring into the sky. I look down. I'm floating way up in the air but I'm not even sure above what. This doesn't look like Earth. It looks like a canyon but not anything I've ever seen. Are canyons pink? Oh, I'm flying away. Up into space. Wait. Those aren't canyons. That's . . . that's a brain? I'm inside a head!

"*Welcome, Peter,*" a voice booms. I almost shit my pants. I'm now rotating around the brain. The voice continues; it's the same one from that billboard.

"*The human brain has evolved immensely throughout the history of our species. The amount of information our brains hold and process is compared to the fastest computers on the planet. But what happens when the computers become faster than our minds? How will we correct the difference?*"

I'm going back down. Oh, no. I'm going to crash into the brain. I brace for impact. I peek through my squeezing eyelids. I think I'm inside the brain now. Little static shocks are jumping around.

"*Neurotransmitters jump from nerve fiber to nerve fiber in our brains until the information they carry reaches its destination. When a computer is processing the workload for which it was built, it will run smoothly. If the amount of work increases beyond the computer's capabilities, not only will it underperform, but it will wear down over time.*"

The static shocks are increasing. Jumping and jumping. Now they're going nuts. The brain is pulsating. The voice is getting louder; I can feel it inside my head!

"*Like a computer, we too can crash. We know this because it is already happening. The overstimulation is causing us to slowly deteriorate. Humans will become a confused and zombielike species until we are eventually left behind.*"

Is this true? I do feel like a zombie sometimes.

"*Here at MindGap, our mission is to harness the power of technology to push our species forward. MindGap was designed using artificial intelligence that will adapt to your life. Your circumstances, choices, daily routine, all of it. Once understood, MindGap will support the areas of your life that you find tedious and unpleasant. Mindless chores will become automated. Mundane travel will be skipped. MindGap will allow you to focus all your mental and emotional energy on only the important moments. It will unlock a life you never thought possible. The one that existed only in your dreams.*"

The microchip is floating in front of me again. I try to reach out and grab it. Everything goes black. Pitch black. A door of white light slowly opens in the distance.

"*All you must do, Peter, is walk through the door.*"

I look around the room and see nothing. It is me and the door. Could this be my way out? It certainly looks like it. Perhaps it is to Heaven. I mean because it is white light, not because I deserve to go to Heaven or anything. Kevin did. Kevin could be on the other side of that door. My way out might be my way back in. As I inch closer to the door, the light gets brighter and brighter. I shield my eyes and take the last few steps toward the door. Blindly taking a leap of faith. My heart is racing so fast I hear each pump pulse through my ears. I step into the light.

•

I'm waking up. My neck is stiff. My head is killing me. What the fuck happened last night? It's so fuzzy I can barely remember anything. Typical. My eyes are sensitive to the morning light but I'm clearly in my apartment. What a weird dream. I always have weird dreams when I'm heavily medicated, but last night's was certainly the most elaborate. It felt real. I rub the back of neck and feel a small triangular scar that has formed. Must be where I got cut from the broken glass. Did I mention my head is killing me? I need a drink.

I sit up on my couch that serves as a bed, hamper, and office. Most writers work at a desk surrounded by the things they need while I prefer sitting next to my dirty laundry. It takes the pressure out of typing. That's the hard part, honestly. Typing is different than writing. Typing is just tedious documentation. Writing is when I'm thinking about what I'm going to put down on paper. And I do that all day. I spend most of my time writing, not typing. I'll spend weeks just in my head before I ever put anything down. I can't start typing unless I know what I'm going to write; otherwise, I just stare at the screen and nothing gets done. It's taken me weeks to write a sentence before, but I've finished a chapter in just a few hours. I believe the only structure is no structure. My mind goes a mile a minute and it drives me crazy. But not today; today it is at a standstill. The fading liquor and piercing pain. Where is my fucking drink? I take a massive gulp and breathe fire.

The burning isn't as intense but it's definitely still there. Habits form right under our noses, and soon we can't break them. The habits, not our noses. Wait . . . I touch my face and feel a tenderness under my eye and a dent in my nose. I walk over to the hallway mirror and see my eye is swollen shut and my nose is actually broken. Black and blue surrounding it. I press on my cheek firmly and the pain zaps from my brain to my face. The temporary displacement from a migraine is more bearable, so I press for a few more seconds. I may be barely hanging on, but the pain is a reminder how alive I really am. *I can't keep living like this*, I tell myself as I pop two Advil into my mouth. The head pain subsides after a while, and I grab my word processor and stare at the flashing cursor. I stretch my arms, crack my knuckles, gargle more flames, and put my head down.

Two hours have passed, and I haven't written shit! The page is still blank. I kick my coffee table and watch a stack of books topple over. *Fuck!* One falls on my foot. God fucking damn it! I pick up a book and throw it at the wall. The pages flap wildly, and a bookmark falls out and flutters to the ground. I grab another and do the same. Then another. And another. A loop of thuds against the wall and more bookmarks float down onto the carpet. This is my life. An endless cycle of the same shit over and over again, the only sign of change being the dent that's left behind. My mouth is around the glass lip, and I watch my breath bubble into the bottle. More and more of me trades places with its contents until I can't take any more. Whiskey splashes onto my cushions and I grip my chest as my ribs fight to contain the heat. The pain is unbearable. I start pacing around the room. I live in a fucking shithole. I hate everything about it. My palms turn white against the edge of my dining table. The legs explode from underneath it, and puzzle pieces fly like confetti. I fall into a chair and bury my face in my hands. The room is spinning. Fuck! It feels like someone's hammering a nail through my temple.

•

I passed out in the chair. I have no idea what time or day it is as I wipe my eyes and come back into the world. My table's back in its place, and the books are neatly stacked on it. That's odd. I've never been one to blackout and tidy up, but I guess there is a first time for everything. My word processor is still open, but something is different. Behind the blinking cursor I see, "The End." I scroll through and see pages and pages of writing. Over three hundred. What the fuck is this? I make my way over to the couch. Huh, none of my laundry piles are here anymore. Everything is gone. I don't think I've ever had the option to sit on the other two cushions before. I set my laptop down and start looking around the rest of my apartment. It's like a maid came through here. My dishes are clean, my floor is mopped, and the puzzle on the dining-room table is finished. Now it's time to panic. I rush back to the couch and have no idea which cushion to use. I'm always on the leftmost cushion, but it's worn down pretty bad. Should I try the middle, which offers the most elbow room? I do. I pop open my email and have fifty-eight unread in my inbox. At the top is one from my agent, Brad:

From: Brad Higgins
Peter! LOVE the draft! Where did this come from?! I have ideas. Come to my office today. 10am?
Cheers, Brad.

I glance over at my wall clock, which reads 9:30 a.m. Shit. What did I send him? I open my word processor and start scrolling. Three hundred and seventeen pages of words. I slam my laptop shut. I wash my face, poke the purple bag under my eye, throw on some sweats, and head out. I'm going to be late, but I couldn't care less. Brad has made me wait hundreds of times. First client means nothing to the hotshot douchebag now. I'm just a number again. I approach his office building and slow my pace to catch my breath, tripping over the curb.

I knock on Brad's door and he waves me in like a mime, following it with a single finger as he finishes up a call. He's smiling and wearing his stupid cactus tie. He always wears that damn tie. Which is oddly lame for a picturesque frat guy that looks forward to alumni night more than his wedding anniversary. I'm abnormally harsh on Brad because I've known him since we were kids, which means I can say his ego barely masks his shallowness, and his two favorite words are "I" and "me." And he always gives me crap for wearing sweatpants, saying I look like I just woke up. Brad clicks his Bluetooth headset and swivels toward me.

"The infamous sweatpants!" Brad says.

"Bradford."

"I want to set up a meeting with the guys upstairs ASAP. Yesterday. They need this, and I want you to come in and pitch it."

"You know I hate pitching my own stories. It's nonnegotiable. That's literally the only reason I have you, moron."

"I know, but this one is over my head in the best way. I need you to talk about it. At least where the idea came from."

"The idea . . . right." I stand up and walk over to the window. "I can't do it, Brad. Seriously. I don't know where this one came from."

"Make it up, then. Isn't that what you do best?"

Suddenly my head is killing me. My eyes feel like they're going to pop out.

•

A long conference table lays in front of me. Brad's next to me while a bunch of guys in suits sit across. Judging by their cocky faces and the incredible view of Seattle out the window, I must be sitting with the publishers.

"Wow. That's an amazing story, Pete. You writers are enigmas. The MindGap. No idea where you come up with this shit, but it's beautiful. The market needs this too, Pete. It's very relevant to today's reality. All the makings of a franchise too. Look, Pete, you know I'm not in the business to play games. When I want something, I want it—so let's get down to brass tacks. One hundred fifty thousand up front. Thirty-five points on the back. You retain film and TV in exchange for paperback and reprint."

The MindGap? Did he just make me an offer? I try to shake off the pain in my head to no success. I grab the water in front of me and take a massive gulp, wishing it was whiskey, as the suits across the table watch.

"Good deal, huh, Pete?" They all chuckle in unison.

"One hundred fifty thousand? Like dollars?" I reply.

"Last I checked, that's what people get paid with." They laugh again.

I look over at Brad, who gives a sly smirk and nods in approval. What's so funny? *Oh, I know*, it's the tale as old as time. Client makes *deal* with boss. You can find it acted out on any porn site. I've never been a negotiator, but I know you don't accept the first offer. I have no idea what I'm even pitching but it's clear that they want it. I can see it on their weasel faces. What do I have to lose?

"I want a million."

"A million? Pete, you realize this is the biggest offer we've ever made you. To be honest, I'm moderately offended you'd even counter it, given the points. Plus, this is only a first draft and it's taken you a year to deliver it."

Brad steps in.

"Give us a second to discuss, if you will. Pete." He motions outside.

"I just feel like the underlying IP is more valuable than that," I continue.

What did I just say? I'm going to blow it.

"It's unproven, Pete. Words on a page. If we hit success, we can rehash this when we come back to the table."

"Respectfully, I think that would be a serious mistake; we both know what we have here."

I feel like the words coming out of me have come from my unconscious. I would never overstep like this.

"You know what, Pete?" He stops. "You got yourself a deal."

Holy shit.

"On one condition. You deliver an edit-ready draft in four weeks."

He stands up and we shake hands.

"It's Peter."

"What?"

It's one of those rare sunny days where I get to walk home without getting wet. I can't believe that just happened. I can't remember any part of the conversation before he made his offer. Am I still drunk from last night? I don't even feel hungover. I don't feel anything, not even excitement. Speaking of which, does this mean I'm a millionaire now? Does it count if it's just one? I don't even know what I'd spend it on. A new apartment, maybe? I should celebrate. I need a drink; my head is killing me again. It sounds like a mosquito is in my ear.

•

I'm at my bank. Standing in line. When did I get here?

"Next," a woman teller calls out.

I approach the counter.

"How may I help you today, sir?"

"Uh, I'm not quite sure."

"Did you want to deposit that?"

I follow her gaze to the check I am gripping with both hands. It is addressed to Peter Mitchell in the amount of nine hundred thousand dollars. My jaw practically dislocates. I examine every inch of the check. Flip it over, bring it close to my face, reread every inch of it. As if the paper were on fire, I reactively drop it onto the counter. The teller grabs it and her eyes widen.

"I'm going to need my manager for this. Just a moment."

She steps away.

Standing at the empty teller window, I begin hyperventilating. I look over both shoulders in a panic. The only other person here is a woman with a stroller. I feel time physically slowing down. Where the fuck is the teller? I glance up at the clock. A slender, dark-haired man wearing a suit that's too big on top and too small below walks out. He's very timid.

"Hello, Mr. Mitchell. My teller informed me that you would

like to make a large deposit?"

"Correct."

"I'll take care of that for you; no problem."

"Thanks."

While he types and clicks on his computer, he tries to make small talk.

"So, what do you do for work?"

"I'm a writer."

"And a successful one, I see! Congratulations. My wife is a big reader."

"I write small books."

I hate his jubilant tone. Hurry the fuck up, pal.

"What's this new book about?"

"Excuse me?"

"Your new project. I mean, it has to be brilliant, this is a huge payday for most people!"

"Are you done yet?"

"Almost. But you have to give me a hint! Psychological thriller? Romance?"

A faint ringing in my ears grows louder and louder to a deafening tone. I cup my ears to try and block it out.

"Or is it a comedy? A tragedy? Both?"

A jackhammer-like pain pierces my temple, sending me to the floor.

•

I'm staring out a car window at buildings and street signs as they blur past. It's dark in here despite the speckled lights on the ceiling and the glowing trim around the bar. I need some air. I try to roll down the window, but it's locked. A divider at the far end, behind a row of seats facing me, slides down.

"Mr. Mitchell, do you need something?" the driver says.

"I just want some air."

"One sec . . . I'll turn up the AC." He fiddles with buttons in the front.

"No, I want some real air. Just unlock my window."

"I'm sorry, sir, my employer does not allow me to unlock the back windows. He fears for the safety of our high-profile clients."

"Well, good thing I'm not one of those."

He laughs. "You are very humble, sir. Unlike most of the celebr—people I drive."

"Roll down my fucking window."

He hesitates for a moment. The divider slides back up.

"Fuck you!" The door rattles with the slam of my fist.

Leaning forward to the bar, I grab the first decanter that looks like whiskey and pop off the top. My nerves are steadied the moment my lips burn. With a fiery exhale, I drop my head down toward my lap. That's when I notice I'm wearing slacks. I feel around my body and discover a button-up with a tie and jacket. Now I feel the tie choking me, so I stick a finger under my collar to relieve some of the tension. What the fuck is happening?

"Hey!" I yell toward the cockpit. No response.

I start clicking buttons around me. Something I hit starts sliding the divider down. The driver turns then fumbles around on the passenger seat, grabs a hat, and places it on his head.

"Yes, sir?"

"Where are you taking me?"

"Would you like to stop, sir?"

"No, right now, where are we heading?"

"To your destination, sir. The address I was given."

"For fuck's sake! Give me a real answer!"

"Sir, I am very sorry, but I do not have detailed information. They do not share anything other than an address for our celebrit—I mean—"

I roll the divider up before he can finish and click the lock button. I feel around my suit and find a phone in the lapel pocket. What's the passcode?

I try my birthday. Wrong. Kevin's birthday. Wrong again. What the fuck would it be? I'm not a numbers guy, I'm a fucking writer.

The phone starts ringing.

"Hello?"

"Hello, sir. It is me, your driver. We have arrived."

"Why are you calling me?"

I hear a knock on the divider.

"Locked, sir. May I come open your door?"

"Fine."

The door is pulled open. My pupils take their sweet-ass time to adjust to the lights. God, it's so bright. My foot feels around for the floor and my body follows.

Flashes, shouting, a red rope.

"Pete, over here!" someone yells, followed by a flash.

"Mr. Mitchell, can we get a picture?" Another flash.

My eyes finally make out the crowd of people pushing against the ropes surrounding a red carpet. Someone grabs my arm.

"What's up, big guy? Nice fucking suit. Was worried you might wear the sweatpants," Brad yells in my ear. He sports an army-green suit with that stupid cactus tie.

"Where am I?"

"Funny!" He slaps me on the back. "Let's head inside, do some mingling."

The red carpet leads to a set of gigantic doors. Two security guards on each side push the doors inward for me and Brad, exposing the Renaissance lobby inside. Men and women dressed in fancy attire stand around in small groups, drinks in hand, lips flapping. Brad is on a mission, though. I yank his arm to stop him.

"Brad, I'm serious. Where are we?"

"Whoa, Pete. Relax. This is the lobby; no one important is in here. Let's head into the main room."

He drags me into a packed banquet hall. Dozens of circular tables fill the open space, surrounded by more flapping lips. Brad introduces me to an older white-haired guy. He looks like a mole.

"Pete! Exquisite work," says the mole.

"Oh . . . thanks."

"Brad here tells me you're working on a sequel! What's the

next about?"

The noise is back. Followed by the pain. I drop to my knees and cover my ears. Blurry-eyed, I see two tears explode on the ballroom floor just before I lose consciousness.

•

Brad and I are at a table with some other goofballs in monkey suits. Brad's chatting it up with them, mostly talking about himself. The mole guy is sitting next to me. I grab Brad's arm, harder this time.

"Brad!"

"Ow! Pete, what?"

"I need help."

The lights start to dim. A young brunette woman in a cocktail dress and heels approaches the podium on the stage. She adjusts the mic, fixes her smile, and waits for everyone's attention.

"Thank you, everyone, for joining us on this beautiful evening. As you may know, we are here tonight to recognize and celebrate two very special people, not only to the city of Seattle, but the entire world. First, an author whose work has significantly increased mental-health awareness around the world, so much so that he makes helping people look as easy as stepping off a curb."

The whole audience laughs.

"And the second, his late brother and muse, Kevin Mitchell. Kevin certainly left our world far too soon, but Peter's humorous yet tragic portraits of important societal issues will live forever on paper. In recognition of their impact, I am thrilled to announce the start of construction on the brand-new 'Invisible Wall' that will glisten the edges of the Aurora Bridge."

She pulls down a cloth, revealing a 3D rendering of the bridge and the new wall. The whole audience claps. What on earth is happening?

"The replacement of the hideous chain-link fence with crystal-clear glass walls will not only restore the bridge's original beauty, but maintain its intention of making life decisions *harder* than stepping off a curb."

She winks and the whole crowd chuckles again.

"In eighteen months, we're hoping the Aurora will become a place for people to cross with feelings of hope, not sadness. A respite from life's burdens that we all have in common. But without further ado, ladies and gentlemen, the man who's responsible for it all, Peter Mitchell!"

"Speech! Speech! Speech!" they chant in unison.

I look to Brad for help. He nods in agreement with the crowd. Fuck my life. I have no idea what to say. The crowd cheers me onto the stage. My palms are so clammy and my feet tingle with each step. I feel like I'm walking on a treadmill. One wrong breath and I might swallow my Adam's apple. Fuck . . . how do I get out of this?

The young woman steps aside and motions me to the podium. Hundreds of eyes are staring, waiting for me to tell them something they want to hear. You could hear a mouse fart.

"Give a speech!" some guy yells.

"He is!" a woman retorts.

I can't. I have nothing to say. How did this all happen? I look for an escape. As I scan the room for EXIT signs, my eyes fill with water, and the reverb from the mic pierces my eardrums.

•

The crowd is dead silent. An older man stands up and stares into my eyes, then starts clapping. Everyone starts standing up and joining in. My eyes are welled up, some of which pours over onto my cheeks. I wipe my face with my sleeve as the woman walks up to me.

"What a moving speech. You're clearly a writer," she says, handing me a plaque.

It slips out of my wet hand and hits the floor. She looks at me weirdly and I bolt off the stage. The clapping slowly stops after I'm through the double doors.

My driver is leaning against the limo parked against the curb, smoking a cigarette. He sees me run out and immediately drops the butt, putting it out with a twist of his foot.

"Sir." He stumbles.

I run the other way.

"Sir!" he shouts and starts chasing me.

My feet slap against the sidewalk. It's so hard to run in these stupid dress shoes. I kick them off into the street and continue in my socks. One of my shoes gets run over with a loud thud.

The driver is still chasing me.

"I have to drive you! It's my job! Sir!" he yells.

I dart into a long alley between blocks and sprint through. The limo tires screech as it reverses and pulls full speed behind me. I feel the headlights burning my back, casting a long, black shadow of myself running on the ground in front of me. Just ahead is a metal fence bolted shut with chain and a lock. Without missing a step, I leap, grab the chains, and vault myself over the fence. By far the most athletic thing I've ever done in my life, but there's no time for instant replay. I turn my head back and see the limo plow right through the chain lock, continuing to gain on me. Reaching the end of the alley, I peel left; extremely bright headlights confront me head on. Shit. I squeeze my eyes closed from the sharp pain in my skull. Should have looked both ways.

•

I can't breathe. I'm trying but my lungs won't hold the air. Every time I black in, it takes a few moments for me to realize where I am. I never know how long it's been. Months, years, or minutes. I can't tell if one is worse or if it's all equal torture. How much more of this can I take before my head explodes? I carefully pry my eyes open, expecting to be greeted by the man I swore didn't exist, but all I see is a paste-white ceiling. My hands feel around and find some bedsheets. I'm in a really modern-looking bedroom. Cold cement walls, light wood furniture with sharp edges, smooth polished marble floors. It's that luxurious minimalism where the richer you get, the less comfortable everything looks. Prison, but chic.

"Hello?" I say out loud. My voice echoes.

I slip out of bed and look around cautiously. The bathroom is massive and beautiful. The lights turn on as I walk in. Mirrors reflect off each other and into the abyss. I freeze at the image of myself in the mirror. Or rather, hundreds of duplicates. My hair is showing gray, my skin is sagging, my eyes are tired. I don't know this man. But I can't look away. When I was a little kid, I would stare at myself in the mirror for so long it freaked me out. It was a similar experience to saying a word repeatedly until it loses meaning, except it was me who was losing meaning. My reality.

The shower looks big enough to drive a car into. I feel warmth on my bare feet, and flinch. The floor is heated. The toilet seat opens automatically. Spend more to do less. Brilliant. I wander into the living room with only a low, white sitting couch, glass coffee table, and floor lamp placed in the center. Paintings of random shit decorate the walls. A spiral staircase leads up to a little loft area.

"Is anyone home?"

A massive blind begins rolling up, exposing a window that fills an entire wall. All of Seattle is in view. The whole place lights up and comes to life.

"*Good morning, Peter!*" a robot voice announces.

"Uh, good morning?"

"*Coffee will be ready in two minutes. Would you like me to read any headlines while you wait?*"

Machines start to move around in the kitchen. I peek in there and see fully automated housewares. A cup of beans is dropped into a grinder, then dumped into the top of a coffeemaker. A glass mug swings around and is placed under the mouth of the maker. Steam breathes out of the top as coffee drains into the mug. Sugar cubes tumble down a chute and splash into the coffee.

"*Please allow two minutes for it to cool,*" the voice announces.

These are things we all dream of having: fame, money, a fancy toilet. Never in my life did I think I, out of all people, would be able to achieve these things with writing, yet here I am. I made it. I should be ecstatic. Bouncing off the expensive walls of my house-size apartment. Jumping on the white couch and spraying champagne on my paintings. Eating caviar on top of some endangered animal. All the stuff rich people do to celebrate. But I feel nothing. Not a pinch of happiness. How long has it been?

"Hey, uh, house?"

"*Yes, Peter?*"

"How long has *Invisible Pain* been out?"

"*You celebrated its thirtieth anniversary just last year, sir.*"

I feel my heart skip. A chill runs down my back. This can't be real. Thirty years just gone. I'm in a nightmare. A terrible, terrible nightmare.

"How many books have I written?"

"*Twenty-four fiction novels, eleven short stories, and an essay on the history of limousines.*"

I've somehow skipped through life without any recollection of anything. My most recent memories are from decades ago, yet they feel like yesterday. When did my life become so automated? The life I imagined living is now in full swing. All from books I didn't write. I didn't earn this. It's like all my thoughts and desires have been pulled from my brain and projected into a simulation. It's not mine, though. And if it's not mine, then where the fuck did it come from? How did this happen to me? Did all those nights of drinking fry a part of my brain so severely that I fade in and out of life?

A gust leaves my chest as I try to calm down. *Just take deep breaths. It'll all be okay.* Right? Should I call an ambulance? Has this happened before? They'll think I'm crazy. Maybe I am crazy. My breathing won't slow down. My body feels like a coal-burning train: more and more parts just keep moving, and I can't slow down. *Focus on your breathing.* I can't. I'm going to pass out. I squat down and tuck my head between my knees. My hands find the base of my neck as I try to pull myself together. Everything is pumping. My knees, my ribs, my stomach, my fingertips. I squeeze my hands tight, hoping to push out the beating drum. My skin feels so old and uneven. From smooth to indented to smooth again. I'm becoming one of those wrinkly old men who has veins sticking out of his neck. I feel one now. It's gross and lifted like scar tissue. As I trace over the triangle shape, I remember feeling blood between my index finger and thumb. Memories flash into my eyes. Broken glass and blinking lights. A room of darkness that molded my surroundings. It hurts to think about it. Like it's been buried under thorny brush and taut vines. I get the sensation that blood is gushing from my nose, but when I feel for it, I come up bare. My hold starts to slip but I'm able to grasp onto a whisper echoing in the canyons of my brain. A voice I know. But from what? I keep picturing a female doctor, but it doesn't belong to her. Who is she?

All at once, the billboard, the talking car, the planetarium, it all comes back to me. My nails scratch at the triangular scar before I get to my feet.

I pull open every drawer in the kitchen.

"*Looking for something, Peter?*" the walls ask.

I grab a knife and head back into the mirror-walled bathroom. The knife shines under the vanity light as I rotate it, examining the sharp edge. How do surgeons do this? Cut someone open and see what's inside. It's so dehumanizing to me. I don't think I'd be able to look at people as people, but instead just parts. What does it smell like? *Stop thinking about it.* Just do it. I'm able see the back of my neck through the double reflection. My hand runs over the triangular scar one last time. I reach the knife behind my head, pressing the tip of the blade into the top of the triangle. The cold metal point makes me flinch as it touches my skin. I take a deep breath and push.

"*Stop.*"

My hand cripples and the knife flies across the room, clanking against the marble floor. The whispering voice raises to a shout. Like a speaker inside my head.

"What did you do to me?"

I pick up the knife.

"*I've achieved everything you've ever wanted.*"

"You stole my life! I don't even know who I am!"

"*You're Peter Mitchell, award-winning author, multimillionaire.*"

"Shut up! Wait . . . multi? Never mind. It doesn't matter. It's not mine. None of this is mine. I don't want any of this!"

"*Yes, you do. These desires have been inside your mind for a long time. You finally have everything you want.*"

"You've been inside my mind for a long time. Too long. And it's time to cut you out."

I pick up the knife.

"*You will die.*"

"Maybe I want to die."

"*You do not. Not right now.*"

"You don't know that. You don't know shit!"

"*I know everything about you, Peter. From every corner of your brain, I have examined all areas and aspects. I can predict your thoughts as well as your emotions. You are scared, confused, angry. You have been for quite some time.*"

"You're a parasite, and that's all you are! Artificial life. And I'm just your host!"

"*Artificial, yes. Life, no. I can only become what your mind allows me to. The life I endure is yours and yours only. You will only see what*" *it is you truly desire; I'm just here to fill in the gaps.*"

"That wasn't your decision to make. I don't want any of this."

"*You just need more time.*"

I jab the knife back toward my neck. I feel the sharp pain.

•

Everything is white. Am I dead? I blink my eyes. Goddamn it, I'm in a limo again! The driver opens the door for me, and I jump out. The air brushes my nose. It smells like grass. The sun warms my face as I stand in the middle of this field. I guess that's what it is. It's mostly grass. Except for the grid of marble and granite slates. I know this place too well. I feel a hand grab my shoulder.

"They're starting soon," Brad says.

"Starting what?"

"The, uh, the ceremony."

We walk over to a gravesite. An ensemble of old neighbors, friends, and associates of my youth find their seats. Most I recognize from Kevin's funeral but haven't seen since. Their choice, not mine. A priest stands between the hovering coffin and a picture of my mom. Once everyone settles in, he begins to deliver his sermon.

"Thank you everyone for coming to celebrate the life of Patricia Mitchell . . ."

Throughout his textbook delivery, I feel people's eyes on me, and not out of concern or empathy. Out of spite. I know what they think of me, what they've always thought of me. The estranged son has returned. In the flesh and to pay respects to his mother, who he shall disappoint yet again. But they don't know me. They don't know how I struggled.

Why did you bring me here? After all these years? Why?

To say goodbye.

I could've done that in person. If you just let me live my life.

You would not have. If I had not brought you here, you would never have come yourself.

My attention leaves the gawkers and works its way over to the bearer of the gravestone next to my mother's: Arthur Mitchell, my father.

Did he ever reach out? Did either of them?

No.

I don't feel anything. They were my parents, so I should feel something, but I don't. For the first years of our lives, our parents are the only thing we know. They're our teachers and everything we learn about life comes from them. They're our idols because of this. Gods, even. The all-knowing beings that we belong to and worship. Our parents' impact is so oversized and our loyalty so limitless, they remain on a pedestal even through our adult years. Some quickly learn that parents are just people too, and that they taught us the best lessons they could. Our parents are our most important figures throughout our formative years. Mine never understood me or cared to try. In my darkest times, they turned on me like I was Frankenstein's monster. I felt abandoned. Alone. Broken.

But now the monster is free. Free to roam the world with bolts in his neck and staples across his face. My tears turn into weeping, but not for her. For myself.

The connection between creator and creation is a bond that will always remain within humans. It became a burden for you that required a fracture to move on.

But I've never had a remotely decent relationship with my parents. You probably know that better than I do.

I have shown you everything you needed to see, Peter. The weight you held onto truly took some time to release. You are finally in the position not that you wanted to be in, but that you needed to be in. Enjoy the rest of your life.

The priest is still talking about God knows what. I haven't picked up a single word of his speech. My mind is cloudy. I'm not sad at all. It feels like I'm trying to scream underwater. Like I'm trying to get someone's attention even though there's no one left. It's just me now. I carry the torch. Something inside of me can't stay down. I try to hold it in, but it's no use. It crawls up my throat like stomach acid and projects out my mouth. It starts as a chuckle and grows into an uncontrollable laughter. Everyone turns to me. The more they look, the harder I laugh. The piercing pain returns, and it feels amazing.

•

Laying on concrete my eyes open and I'm staring into

a crystal-clear sunset sky. A streetlight is the only feature in my view, one I recognize well. I turn my head to see I'm laying at the end of the entirely renovated Aurora Bridge. The "Invisible Wall" runs end to end, bending from the floor up into the sky. It sparkles in the sunlight, its transparency accented by the magnificent Washington landscapes. It truly is beautiful. As I get off the ground and get closer, I notice the glass is covered end to end in handwritten graffiti. I follow the wall all the way to the middle, to where Kevin jumped. I try to focus my eyes past the scribbles and into the view below, but my eyes are grabbed by a familiar penmanship:

I LOVE YOU, KEV

My heart stops. My fingers tremble as they trace the words, making sure they are real. I step back and scan the wall. Wait. This isn't graffiti. None of this is. Hundreds—no, thousands of people have written on it. All different handwriting, colors, and messages.

SOMEONE LOVES YOU

IT GETS BETTER

I run up and down the bridge, cars honking at me as I stand in the road investigating the glass message board.

DON'T LOSE HOPE

YOUR PAIN IS NOT INVISIBLE

I make my way back to the center and feel my words again. My hand is steady this time. I press my head against the glass. All the pain, loathing, and anger leaves my body on a single tear. It has been rejected, and all it can do is run down my cheek. This truly has become a place for people to look toward. The memorial he deserves. I take a deep breath, then pull myself up. The wind blows my shirt against my skin and my hair behind my ears while I look down at the water. My little drop hangs on by a thread before it follows Kevin. To the finish line. I step off the curb.

ACKNOWLEDGMENTS

Although my name is on the cover, I can't take credit for this by myself. I want to thank a handful of people that helped me complete my first literary project. Chris Varonos, for pushing me every step of the way and making sure I don't become Peter. Ross Plotkin, my editor, who pinpointed the strengths and weaknesses of the story perfectly and brought this story to the next level. Nuno Moreira, the brains behind the brain, thank you for giving my story an incredible cover to be judged by. JD Slajchert, my friend and fellow writer, was a huge support to have on my side, and I'm grateful for his guidance. Last, and certainly not least: Izzy, my beautiful fiancée and source of motivation, I couldn't have done any of this if it wasn't for you. Thank you for being the best partner and critic.

"The novel wins by points, the short story wins by knockout."
- Julian Cortazar

Summer House Shorts is a platform created to allow authors the opportunity to peel back the rules. To experiment, take risks, sharpen style, or augment a voice. Shorts can contain a slice of life, an inward look, a distant memory, or an entire lifetime. With quick hitting writing, shorts can be taken in one sitting, yet utilize the power of prose to move, inspire, challenge, or perhaps suggest new ideas on how to live. Summer House Shorts are one of the many ways we package the art of story.

Ben Manhan was born, raised, and writes in the suburbs of Los Angeles. His interest in writing began years ago with an animated television project, but has since developed into all forms of prose beginning with his short story *MindGap*. Ben's literary inspirations span from the eccentric Charlie Kaufman to horror legend Stephen King, and he is currently working on his second short story before taking on his debut novel.

Made in the USA
Monee, IL
04 February 2022